Dear Parents:

Congratulations! Your child is taking the first steps on an exciting journey. The destination? Independent reading!

STEP INTO READING® will help your child get there. The program offers five steps to reading success. Each step includes fun stories and colorful art or photographs. In addition to original fiction and books with favorite characters, there are Step into Reading Non-Fiction Readers, Phonics Readers and Boxed Sets, Sticker Readers, and Comic Readers—a complete literacy program with something to interest every child.

Learning to Read, Step by Step!

STEP 1

Ready to Read **Preschool–Kindergarten**
• big type and easy words • rhyme and rhythm • picture clues
For children who know the alphabet and are eager to begin reading.

STEP 2

Reading with Help **Preschool–Grade 1**
• basic vocabulary • short sentences • simple stories
For children who recognize familiar words and sound out new words with help.

STEP 3

Reading on Your Own **Grades 1–3**
• engaging characters • easy-to-follow plots • popular topics
For children who are ready to read on their own.

STEP 4

Reading Paragraphs **Grades 2–3**
• challenging vocabulary • short paragraphs • exciting stories
For newly independent readers who read simple sentences with confidence.

STEP 5

Ready for Chapters **Grades 2–4**
• chapters • longer paragraphs • full-color art
For children who want to take the plunge into chapter books but still like colorful pictures.

STEP INTO READING® is designed to give every child a successful reading experience. The grade levels are only guides; children will progress through the steps at their own speed, developing confidence in their reading.

Remember, a lifetime love of reading starts with a single step!

This book is dedicated to all the big people who are helping smaller people learn to read. The StoryBots love you!

Designed by Greg Mako

Visit us on the Web!
StepIntoReading.com
rhcbooks.com

Educators and librarians, for a variety of teaching tools, visit us at RHTeachersLibrarians.com

ISBN 978-0-593-18159-1 (trade) — ISBN 978-0-593-18161-4 (lib. bdg.) —
ISBN 978-0-593-18160-7 (ebook)

Printed in the United States of America
10 9 8 7 6 5 4 3 2 1

STEP 1 READY TO READ

STEP INTO READING®

STORYBOTS®

WHEELS ON THE ROAD

by Scott Emmons

illustrated by Nikolas Ilic and Nelson Boles

Random House New York

Let's take a ride that
is full of surprises.

We will see trucks
and cars in all
shapes and sizes!

It is fun to drive,

but please do it right.

Fasten your seat belt
good and tight.

There are big trucks
and small cars.

Some are fast.

Some are slow.

There are wheels
rolling on roads
everywhere we go.

There are electric cars,
which run on volts,

and junky heaps
of old nuts and bolts.

Here is a truck
that is loaded
with frogs.

And this big old truck hauls happy hogs.

That monster truck roars
as it soars up above.

Ring! Ring! Ring!

The ice cream truck
brings us treats
we all love.

It does not matter
if you are speedy and
new or noisy and slow.

When the engine
is revving,
it is time
to go, go, GO!